Care Bears™

Easter Egg Hunt

By Quinlan B. Lee   Illustrated by Jay Johnson

Designed by Rick DeMonico

ISBN 0-439-69161-3

12 11 10 9 8 7 6 5 4 3 2   5 6 7 8 9/0

Printed in the U.S.A.

First printing, February 2005

SCHOLASTIC INC.

New York   Toronto   London   Auckland   Sydney
Mexico City   New Delhi   Hong Kong   Buenos Aires

Spring was in bloom in Care-a-lot as Funshine Bear
and Tenderheart Bear sat watching the clouds float by.

"Easter's almost here," said Tenderheart Bear. "I can't wait!"

"What's your favorite part of Easter?" Funshine Bear asked. "Oh, that's easy," Tenderheart Bear said. "I love the Easter egg hunt with my friends. Would you like to help me get ready?"

"You bet!" said Funshine Bear.

First, Tenderheart Bear and Funshine Bear
went to the farm to collect eggs for the hunt.
"Look at all the baby chicks," said Tenderheart Bear.
"They're so soft and fuzzy."

"And funny," giggled Laugh-a-lot Bear. "They tickle.
I love how silly and sweet they are."

On the way back to Care-a-lot Castle Tenderheart Bear
and Funshine Bear met Cheer Bear.
"Would you like to help dye the eggs?" they asked her.

"I'd love to! Coloring eggs is my favorite part of Easter,"
cheered Cheer Bear. "There's red, yellow, blue, purple—
every color of the rainbow!"

"All finished!" said Cheer Bear, placing the last colored egg in the bucket. "Now all we need are the treats."

Funshine Bear rubbed his tummy. "Mmmm . . . jelly beans, marshmallow bunnies, and chocolate eggs. All the sweet treats are the best part of Easter."

"We better get going," said Tenderheart Bear.
"It's almost time for the hunt."

"You're right," said Funshine Bear. "All of our friends
will be here soon with their Easter baskets."

Funshine Bear and Tenderheart Bear quickly hid treats here and there throughout the Cloud Patch.

Funshine Bear found a little garden of spring flowers.
He put an egg-stra special treat behind their smiling faces.

"The hunt is my favorite part of Easter," said Champ Care Bear as he gathered all the other Care Bears together on a rainbow.

"On your mark, get set, go!"
"Happy hunting, everyone!" cheered Good Luck Bear.

The Care Bears looked under clouds and peeked around stars,
shouting and laughing as they found all the eggs and treats.

Soon their baskets were almost full.

Way in the corner of the Cloud Patch, Share Bear spotted something in the garden. She ran over and gently lifted the leaves of the flowers.

"Look what I found!" she cried. "A big chocolate bunny!"

All the Care Bears came running to see Share Bear's special find.

"Wow!" said Tenderheart Bear. "I know for sure what you like best about Easter—finding the chocolate bunny!"

"Close," replied Share Bear. "But actually, my most egg-stra special part of Easter is sharing it with all of you."